Not Yet, Zebra

Lou Kuenzler   Julia Woolf

ff

FABER & FABER

Annie said to the animals,
"Please stand in a line.
I'm painting my **alphabet**.
Come one at a time!

"First **A**ardvark and **B**ear, and **C**rocodile too.

"Not yet, Zebra. I'm not ready for you.
You're not the one I want to see.

Z comes at the end. We've only reached D.

"Now Dog and Elephant and ...

"Zebra, please think.

You are **NOT** Flamingo. You are not even pink!

"I need Gorilla and Hamster and ...

What did I say?
Not yet, Zebra. Please go away!

"Now **I**guana.

Then **J**ellyfish.

"Then Kangaroo.

"And Lion and Monkey must have a go too.

"N is quite tricky...

"But you're **DEFINITELY** not **N**ewt...
I know you're just Zebra wearing a suit!

"O is for ... Oh no!

"Zebra, not yet!
Don't you know your alphabet?"

Annie sighed and said firmly, "Octopus is O.
Stop pulling her legs and PLEASE let her go!

"Panda, Quail, Rhinoceros, come along through.
Let Snake slither in and ... Zebra, just SHOO!

"I know Tiger is stripy ...
but he's not black
and white!

And Unicorn
CERTAINLY
doesn't look right.

"You can't mess about with the **ABC**.
We're still not at **Z**, we've only reached **V** ...
Vulture and **W**alrus, please step forward next.

Now does anyone's name contain an **X**?

"Not yet, Zebra.
You are not Fo**X**.

Don't be so naughty.
Let him out of that **box!**

"Go away, Zebra! Let **Y**ak have his turn.
When are **you** **ever** going to learn?

"Now who do I need? I am right at the end . . .

"Ah, yes!" Annie cried.
"Where's **Z**ebra, my friend . . . ?

"Where has he got to?" Annie looked all around.
But Zebra just simply couldn't be found.

"Strange!" Annie wondered,

"Was it something I said?

I can hear snoring.

Oh no, he's in ...

"...BED!"